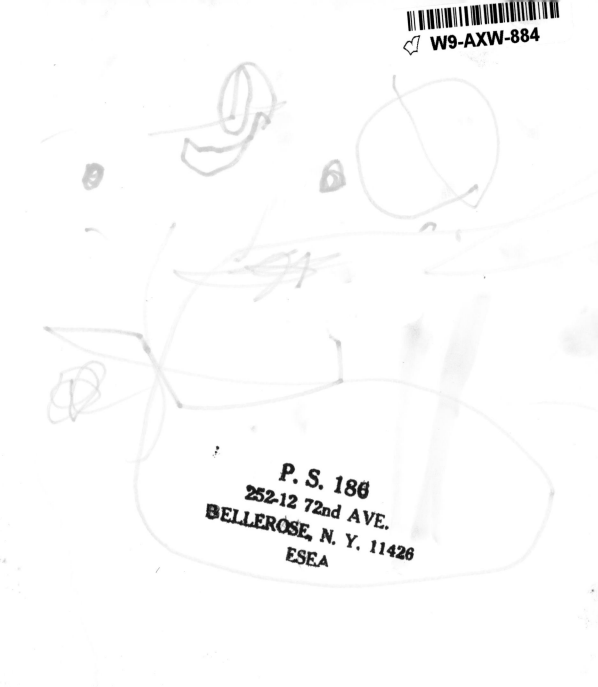

JUST SHOPPING WITH MOM

BY
MERCER MAYER

A Random House PICTUREBACK® Book

Random House **New York**

Just Shopping with Mom book, characters, text, and images © 1989 Mercer Mayer. LITTLE CRITTER, MERCER MAYER'S LITTLE CRITTER, and MERCER MAYER'S LITTLE CRITTER and Logo are registered trademarks of Orchard House Licensing Company. All rights reserved. Published in the United States by Random House Children's Books, a division of Random House, Inc., New York. Originally published in 1989 by Golden Books Publishing Company, Inc. PICTUREBACK, RANDOM HOUSE, and the Random House colophon are registered trademarks of Random House, Inc.
www.randomhouse.com/kids
Educators and librarians, for a variety of teaching tools, visit us at
www.randomhouse.com/teachers
Library of Congress Control Number: 88051568
ISBN-10: 0-307-11972-6   ISBN-13: 978-0-307-11972-8
Printed in the United States of America
18 17 16
First Random House Edition 2006

We went shopping.

We went to the food store.
I got to push the cart.

It was heavy,
but not too heavy.

"I want to ride," said my little sister.
"Don't you think you are too big to ride?" asked Mom.

"No," said my little sister.
I had to push her, too. Then the cart was very heavy.

But she ate it.
I think Mom was mad.

My little sister grabbed a big bag of candy.
Mom said, "Not today."

Mom said, "Stay here. I will be right back."

I turned around and
my little sister was gone.

I looked and looked, but I didn't know where she could be.

I found her back at the candy.
I tried to make her come with me.
She said, "No!"
Then Mom found both of us.
I think she was mad.

My little sister said, "I want candy."
Mom said, "I told you, no candy today.
Would you like to go to time-out instead?"

We walked by some books.
We each got to pick out one.

We walked by some toys.
My little sister said,
"I want the yellow duck."
Mom said, "You don't need
the yellow duck."

"I really need a red pail,"
said my little sister.
"No!" said Mom.

Mom wanted paper towels.
My little sister pulled out a roll from
the bottom of the pile.

Everything fell down.
The man who owned the store
didn't look too happy.

Mom paid for everything.
We took the food to the car. My little sister said,
"I want ice cream."
I said, "I want ice cream, too."
Mom said, "Not now. We have another place to go."
We walked back to the mall.

We passed by the bakery.
My little sister said, "I want cake."
"Not today," said Mom.

We passed by the pet store.
"I want a kitty," said my little sister.
"But you already have a kitty," said Mom.

We passed by the toy store.
"I want a doll," said my little sister.
"No," said Mom. "You need a new dress."

We walked into the dress store.
Mom picked out a dress.
My little sister tried it on.

Mom said, "Doesn't she look sweet?"
I said, "Yes."

Mom bought the dress.
Then we all went to get an
ice-cream cone...finally.
That was the best part.

8961